ONE WILD
CHRISTMAS

To Chloe, Erik and Sarah

Text and illustrations © 2019 Nicholas Oldland

Kids Can Press gratefully acknowledges the financial support of the Government of Ontario, through Ontario Creates; the Ontario Arts Council; the Canada Council for the Arts; and the Government of Canada for our publishing activity.

Published in Canada and the U.S. by Kids Can Press Ltd.
25 Dockside Drive, Toronto, ON M5A 0B5

Kids Can Press is a Corus Entertainment Inc. company

www.kidscanpress.com

The artwork in this book was rendered in Photoshop.
The text is set in Animated Gothic.

Edited by Yvette Ghione
Series design by Marie Bartholomew
Designed by Michael Reis

Printed and bound in Malaysia in 3/2019 by Tien Wah Press (Pte) Ltd.

CM 19 0 9 8 7 6 5 4 3 2 1

Library and Archives Canada Cataloguing in Publication

Title: One wild Christmas / written and illustrated by Nicholas Oldland.
Names: Oldland, Nicholas, author, illustrator.
Identifiers: Canadiana 20190042451 | ISBN 9781525302039 (hardcover)
Classification: LCC PS8629.L46 O54 2019 | DDC jC813/.6—dc23

ONE WILD CHRISTMAS

Nicholas Oldland

Kids Can Press

But when they turned their attention to trimming the Christmas tree, they suddenly realized that they had forgotten the most important decoration of all!

Putting up lights ...

And wrapping presents.

Everything had to be done to perfection.

On their first Christmas Eve together, the three friends were busy preparing food ...

Hanging their stockings ...

There once was a bear, a moose and a beaver whose very favorite time of year was Christmas.

Quickly, the moose and the beaver rushed out
into the forest. The bear followed close behind.

First they came across
a maple tree ...

TOO SMALL.

Next they saw
a birch tree ...

Finally, they found a pine tree. It was sweet-smelling,
had long soft needles and was just the right size.

But to the bear's horror, the beaver went to chop down the tree.

The bear loved all living things, especially trees.
And this was the most beautiful tree he had ever seen.

The three friends had a big problem. There was no way the
bear would let the beaver and the moose harm this tree.

And the beaver and the moose were not about to let the bear get in the way of their perfect Christmas tree ...

It was a short argument. The moose and the beaver were no match for the bear's strength.

The bear was happy the tree was safe, but he worried
that his love of trees might ruin their Christmas.

Then he had an idea.

The bear grabbed his sled
and raced home.

Back at the cabin, the bear gathered all of the food, decorations and presents ...

And carefully loaded
everything onto his sled.

The bear's journey back proved a little more difficult.

The moose and the beaver were relieved to see their friend. And as soon as they saw the sled loaded with presents, food and Christmas decorations, they knew exactly what the bear had in mind.

Together the friends set up a table with all the food ...

Arranged their stockings ...

Hung the ornaments ...

And placed the presents under the tree.

Then when they were all done, they had a snowball fight.

At last the bear, the moose and the beaver were ready to celebrate. Not only did they agree that this tree was perfect, it was also the perfect Christmas.